A BOY, A DOG,
A FROG and
A FRIEND

by Mercer

and Marianna Mayer

DIAL BOOKS FOR YOUNG READERS
New York

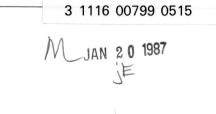
Published by Dial Books for Young Readers
A division of E. P. Dutton | A division of New American Library
2 Park Avenue, New York, New York 10016
Copyright © 1971 by Mercer and Marianna Mayer. All rights reserved.
Library of Congress Catalog Card Number: 70-134857
Printed in Hong Kong by South China Printing Co.
COBE
10 12 14 15 13 11

For crazy Dina